Barbie™
The Pearl Princess

Adapted by Mary Tillworth
Based on the screenplay by Cydne Clark & Steve Granat
Illustrated by Uklutay Design Group

Special thanks to Diane Reichenberger, Cindy Ledermann, Jocelyn Morgan, Tanya Mann, Julia Phelps, Sharon Woloszyk, Rita Lichtwardt, Carla Alford, Renee Reeser Zelnick, Rob Hudnut, David Wiebe, Shelley Dvi-Vardhana, Gabrielle Miles, Rainmaker Entertainment, Walter P. Martishius, and Sarah Lazar

A GOLDEN BOOK · NEW YORK

Published in the United States by Golden Books, an imprint of Random House Children's Books, a division of Random House LLC, 1745 Broadway, New York, NY 10019, and in Canada by Random House of Canada Limited, Toronto, Penguin Random House Companies. No part of this book may be reproduced or copied in any form without permission from the copyright owner. Golden Books, A Golden Book, A Little Golden Book, the G colophon, and the distinctive gold spine are registered trademarks of Random House LLC.
randomhouse.com/kids
Educators and librarians, for a variety of teaching tools, visit us at RHTeachersLibrarians.com
ISBN 978-0-385-37305-0
Printed in the United States of America
10 9 8 7 6 5 4 3

Once upon a time, in the magical underwater kingdom of Seagundia, a mermaid princess was born. The baby had a magical power only found within the royal family. She could make pearls move and dance and glow, all without touching them!

Everyone loved the princess—everyone except the king's brother-in-law, Caligo. Now that there was an heir to the throne, Caligo's son, Fergis, would never be crowned king. So Caligo came up with an evil plan. . . .

Caligo paid a mean, old mermaid named Scylla to do away with the mermaid princess. But when Scylla saw the baby, she fell in love with her. Knowing that the princess would never be safe with Caligo around, Scylla took the child and fled from the palace. The king and queen were heartbroken.

Scylla named the princess Lumina and raised her
in a hidden cave far from the mermaid kingdom.
She told Lumina nothing of her past and pretended
to be her aunt. Although Scylla loved to watch the
child play with pearls, she knew that Lumina had to
keep her magic a secret. Caligo had spies everywhere,
and they knew about the princess's rare gift.

Years passed, and Lumina grew into a beautiful young mermaid. She loved to pretend to be a princess with her sea horse friend, Kuda.

"Do you think we'll ever get to see the castle?" Lumina asked.

"Maybe someday," replied Kuda.

One day, Murray, an eel who worked for Caligo, arrived at the cave. He gave Scylla an invitation to a royal ball in honor of Fergis, who was going to be named heir to the throne. The eel then told Scylla that Caligo needed her to poison the king at the ball so that Fergis could take the crown sooner than expected.

When Scylla refused, Murray threatened that Caligo would tell everyone how she had done away with the princess if she didn't do as he said. Reluctantly, Scylla agreed.

Lumina wanted to go to the royal ball, too. But Scylla knew that the princess might be recognized if she left the cave. So Scylla packed her bag and kissed Lumina good-bye.

But Scylla forgot her invitation, so Lumina and Kuda decided to journey to Seagundia to bring it to her. This was their big chance to see the castle!

On their way, Lumina and Kuda met
a lonely stonefish named Spike who had
poisonous spikes. Lumina believed in leaving
things a little better than she found them, so
she used her pearl magic to place a beautiful
pearl on the end of each pointy
tip. Soon Spike, Lumina, and
Kuda were good friends.

After swimming through a deep kelp
forest and battling dangerous vampire squids,
Lumina, Kuda, and Spike finally made it
to the mermaid kingdom. Lumina couldn't
believe how beautiful the palace was!

Suddenly, Lumina and Kuda were pulled into a
beauty salon by an orange-haired octopus. Madame
Ruckus, the salon's owner, thought Lumina was
her new stylist. Before she knew it, Lumina had been
put to work styling a young mermaid's hair.

Secretly using her magic, Lumina wove sparkling pearls into the mermaid's hair. The mermaid gasped when she saw her new, unique hairdo. "That is so totally awesome!" she cried as she showed her friends.

Lumina quickly became the most popular stylist in the salon.

Lumina loved her new job. Through her styling, she was able to leave her customers a little better than she had found them! And then she learned a wonderful surprise— the entire salon staff had been invited to the royal ball!

The royal ball was more dazzling than anything Lumina had ever seen. Scalloped chandeliers hung from the ceiling, and the king and queen sat on an ornate throne.

As Lumina floated down the grand staircase, everyone turned to stare at the beautiful mermaid and her glittering pink gown covered in glowing pearls.

Meanwhile, hidden in a corner of the ballroom, Caligo watched with evil delight as Scylla mixed poison into the king's drink. "You rid me of one pest many years ago—now you'll rid me of another!" he told Scylla.

Scylla did not want to poison the king, but she had to obey to keep Lumina safe from Caligo.

Finally, it was time for a royal toast to Fergis. Reluctantly, Scylla presented the king with the poisoned drink. As the king raised the glass, she had a change of heart. She frantically tried to take the glass away from the king, but Caligo stopped her.

"I put poison in the king's cup!" Scylla cried when the king was about to drink.

As Scylla revealed Caligo's treachery, Caligo removed a pearl from one of Spike's poisoned spikes—and pushed Scylla right into the tip!

Using her magic, Lumina created a whirlpool
around Caligo and trapped him in a pearl prison.
Then she rushed to Scylla's side.

Lumina quickly asked Spike if there was a cure for his poison.

"The only one I know of is the Sulfer Lily," said Spike. Luckily, Fergis's true dream had never been to become king. He wanted to be a botanist! Fergis took the flower from his collection and put two petals on Scylla's wound. Slowly, Scylla opened her eyes—she was cured!

"You have the royal gift—the pearl magic," said the king. Scylla explained how she had taken Lumina years ago to keep her safe from Caligo.

Fergis placed the Pearl of the Sea medallion around Lumina's neck, and suddenly Lumina's tail turned purple to gold and her dress transformed into a pearlescent gown.

"I can't believe it—I'm really a princess!" Lumina exclaimed. As the kingdom celebrated the return of their long-lost princess, Lumina knew that she had finally found her family and her true home. She was the Pearl Princess.